To my lovely and loveable Anna – J.H.

To Frej – my happy little chap! – B.G.

First published 2006 by Walker Books Ltd
87 Vauxhall Walk, London SE11 5HJ

10 9 8 7 6 5 4 3 2 1

Text © 2006 Judy Hindley
Illustrations © 2006 Brita Granström

The right of Judy Hindley and Brita Granström to be identified as author and illustrator respectively of this work has been asserted by them in accordance with the Copyright, Designs and Patents Act 1988

This book has been handlettered by the artist

Printed in China

British Library Cataloguing in Publication Data:
a catalogue record for this book is available
from the British Library

ISBN-13: 978-0-7445-9282-5
ISBN-10: 0-7445-9282-8

www.walkerbooks.co.uk

WALKER BOOKS
AND SUBSIDIARIES
LONDON • BOSTON • SYDNEY • AUCKLAND

Baby Talk

A Book of First Words and Phrases

Judy Hindley

illustrated by Brita Granström

Baby in a nappy,
Baby with
a brush.

What's the baby
saying?

Baby with a blanket,
Baby with
a bear.

Baby playing
hide-and-
seek.

Where's
the baby?

There!

Baby in
a fuzzy hat,

Baby in a coat.

Where's the baby going?

The
baby's
going ...

OUT!

Baby on the swings now,
Watch the baby fly.
Baby swinging down low,
Baby swinging high!

Baby climbing up the steps,

Baby sliding down.

Baby sliding off
-bump!

Baby saying
"OWWW!"

There, there, Baby –
Have a little cry –
Have a cuddle,
Have a kiss,
Have another try!

Baby back at home again.

Here's a bowl and spoon.

Where's the baby's dinner?

It's all
gone!

Baby in the mirror – look –
With a funny hat.
Baby with a bubble beard,

Baby
going...

SPLASH!

Baby with a pillow—
What a sleepy-head!
Night-night, Baby,
Baby's gone to bed.

Night-night,

night-night,

night-night...